BIOME BATTLES Book 2

Taking Back the Tundra

by Bob Temple   illustrated by Savannah Horrocks

PICTURE WINDOW BOOKS
Minneapolis, Minnesota

Editor: Jill Kalz
Designers: Nathan Gassman and Hilary Wacholz
Page Production: Melissa Kes
Associate Managing Editor: Christianne Jones
The illustrations in this book were created
with watercolor and ink.

Picture Window Books
5115 Excelsior Boulevard
Suite 232
Minneapolis, MN 55416
877-845-3392
www.picturewindowbooks.com

Library of Congress Cataloging-in-Publication Data
Temple, Bob.
Taking back the tundra / by Bob Temple ;
illustrated by Savannah Horrocks.
p. cm. — (Read-it! chapter books: Biome Battles ; 2)
ISBN 978-1-4048-3648-8 (library binding)
[1. Tundra-Fiction. 2. Prophecies-Fiction.
3. Adventure and adventurers-Fiction. 4. Youths'
art.] I. Horrocks, Savannah, 1935- ill. II. Title.
PZ7.T243Tak 2008
[Fic]-dc22   2007033076

Table of Contents

Taking Back the Tundra

A curious boy who many Imps believe is one of the two humans mentioned in the Imp Prophecy

Ari

Ari's best friend and co-adventurer who many Imps believe is the other human from the Imp Prophecy

Kendra

Troll King

Leader of the Trolls, a group of large, mean, smelly creatures who seek to rule the world by destroying the biomes and turning Earth into a wasteland

Tundra

Rain Forest

Desert

MAP and CHARACTER KEY

Trace

Son of King Crag, the Imp King, and Ari and Kendra's guide through the world's biomes

King Crag

Leader of the Imps, a group of small, gentle creatures who protect all of Earth's biomes from harm

Prairie

Wetlands

IMP VILLAGE

Ocean

A Chill in the Air

Ari lay awake at night, unable to sleep. Many weeks had passed since he and his friend Kendra last saw Trace, the tiny being from the Imp world. Still, Ari couldn't get the adventure out of his mind.

CHAPTER 1

Ari and Kendra's journey with Trace through the rain forest seemed like a dream. But Ari and Kendra knew it was real. Ari had proof. He had a note that Trace had pressed into his palm before disappearing through Ari's bedroom door.

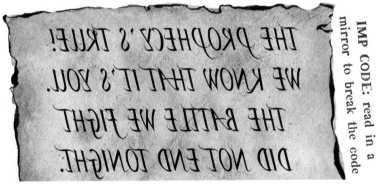

IMP CODE: read in a mirror to break the code

THE PROPHECY'S TRUE!
WE KNOW THAT IT'S YOU.
THE BATTLE WE FIGHT
DID NOT END TONIGHT.

The Imp Prophecy said that a boy and a girl—two humans—would come to the Imps. They would help the Imps save Earth from the evil Trolls once and for all.

The Trolls lived underground. They were unable to survive in sunlight, clean air, and water. They sought to destroy the planet's biomes—to make Earth a wasteland.

They could then rise to the surface and take control of Earth.

Ari knew from Trace's note that the battle they had fought in the rain forest would not be the last. But when would the other battles take place? And where?

So many questions. But one question, more than any other, kept him awake at night: How did Trace know that Ari was the boy from the Imp Prophecy?

Ari just *had* to see Trace again.

But Ari had no way of knowing how or when Trace would come back. Last time, strange noises had come from Ari's closet before Trace arrived. Sadly, those noises had not come back. Every day, Kendra would meet Ari at the bus stop, hoping for exciting news.

"Nope," Ari would say. "Nothing last night. Not a sound. Not a trace."

9

Finally, one night, Ari woke up shivering. He gathered his blankets around him. But the chill still went right through. By morning, he had a runny nose and a cough.

"You don't look so good, Ari," Kendra said at the bus stop. "Really. Are you sick?"

"I must be getting a cold," Ari said, sniffling. "I just couldn't get warm last night."

"But it was hot last night. It felt like the middle of summer!" Kendra said.

"I know," Ari said. "But it was like there was an icy-cold winter wind blowing through my bedroom."

Kendra gasped. "Wait a minute. You had a cold breeze in your room?" she asked. "You don't suppose—"

Before Kendra could finish her sentence, the school bus came around the corner. It headed down the street and pulled up in front of her and Ari. The door swung open, and the two friends climbed aboard.

Suddenly, Ari felt better. "You're right!" he said. "I bet the cold was some kind of sign from Trace. I've been waiting for weeks to hear from him. Kendra, this is going to be a very, *very* long day."

A Long Day

Ari tried hard to pay attention at school.
When he and Kendra passed between
classes, they would nod at each other. Each
knew exactly what the other was thinking.

Was Trace back? If so, where would he take them? It would be someplace cold. The North Pole? The South Pole?

Finally, three o'clock came. Ari and Kendra ran out of school and caught the bus for home.

When the bus pulled up to their stop, they hopped off and ran toward Ari's house.

Ari stumbled on the top step and fell, tearing his pants and scraping the skin on his knees. But he barely noticed the pain. He dug through his backpack for the key.

"Ari," Kendra said, her hand holding the doorknob. "Look at this."

Kendra let go of the knob. A perfect handprint was left behind.

That's when Ari noticed the coating of frost on the outside of the door. The warmth of Kendra's hand had melted a hand-shaped spot on the doorknob.

"It's freezing," Kendra said. "The door is freezing!"

If Ari had any doubts before, he had none now. Trace was back, and he was going to be taking Ari and Kendra on a chilly adventure.

Ari worked the key into the lock as quickly as he could, turned the knob, and pushed hard.

A blast of icy air hit both of them.

Ari dropped his backpack and headed up toward his bedroom. Kendra was right behind him. They both slipped on the ice-covered stairs as they ran to the top.

CHAPTER 2

Ari looked down the hallway and saw exactly what he had hoped to see for so many weeks.

Whoosh! A small, dark figure disappeared through Ari's bedroom door. Kendra gasped. She saw it, too.

Together, without missing a beat, they both said the same word: "Trace."

A Cold New World

Ari and Kendra rushed down the hall.
But when they reached the door to Ari's
bedroom, they stopped. They stared at the
closed door—the door through which Trace
had disappeared.

"When we open this door," Ari said, "my bedroom won't be there."

"Whatever is there," Kendra added, "will be cold."

Ari reached for the doorknob and jerked the door open. Behind it was a flat, frozen

land. Rocks and small shrubs dotted the snowy ground. A large herd of caribou stood off in the distance.

"Tundra," Ari said.

Kendra didn't seem to care what it was. "Let's go!" she said.

She grabbed Ari's hand and stepped through the doorway. Ari came through, too. Just like that, the hallway in Ari's house was no longer behind them.

Ari and Kendra stayed close together as they walked across the strange new land. Thick snow crunched beneath their feet. There wasn't a tree to be seen. Everything, everywhere, was frozen.

Finally, a dark figure darted out of nowhere. It was Trace. Ari quickly knew something was different.

Frost coated the tips of Trace's long, dark hair. He shivered. His face looked different somehow. The sparkle in his eyes was gone.

Trace bent down in front of Ari and cupped his hands over Ari's skinned knees.

Ari felt the pain slowly leave and looked down to see the skin completely healed.

Trace stood up and reached for Kendra's hand. He squeezed it for a moment and then waved for the kids to follow him.

"Are you OK?" Ari asked. "You seem—"

Ari stopped himself. He remembered that Trace could not speak outside the walls of the Imps' village. Trace raised a finger to his lips. It was clear he wanted the kids to be quiet. Again, he waved for them to follow him.

For the next hour, Ari and Kendra walked in silence behind Trace. They wondered all the way what was bothering him. They would find out soon enough.

A King in Need

At last, the three reached a wall. It was
the same wall that had surrounded the
Imp village in the rain forest. This time,

however, it was covered in ice instead of green vines.

Trace moved between Ari and Kendra. He held their hands and walked quickly toward the wall. In an instant, all three friends were through the wall and inside the Imps' village.

It was nothing like Ari and Kendra remembered. The land of Imps merrily playing and singing was gone. Now, it was a frozen land. The waterfall wasn't a gleaming band of water that seemed to come from the sky. It was frozen solid. Not a sound was heard.

Inside the walls of the village, Trace could speak. "Come with me," he said. "My father needs you."

Ari shook his head. "But he doesn't want us to help," Ari said. "He doesn't believe we are the humans from the Imp Prophecy."

"He needs you," Trace said. "Please. Please come and help. For him. For me!"

"Of course!" Kendra said. "If King Crag needs us, we'll help."

Trace led them toward the king's house. Imps peered out from their homes and from around trees and bushes. "They are back," Ari heard one whisper.

Trace opened the door to the king's house. Ari and Kendra ducked to enter. Once inside, they could not believe what they saw.

Although a small figure, King Crag usually carried himself in a big way. This day, however, he lay on the floor of his home, covered in thick blankets. Frost clung to his eyebrows and hair.

"My father," Trace said, shaking his head. "The cold weakens him. He will not survive much longer, unless you help."

Ari and Kendra were confused—and cold. They wrapped themselves in blankets while they sought some answers.

"What happened to the village? Why is it so cold?" Kendra asked. "If the cold weakens your father, why are you all still here?"

"The Trolls," Trace said. "The Trolls have come to the tundra to destroy it. It is our duty as Imps to stop them. If the Trolls succeed, the entire planet is in danger."

Ari and Kendra looked at each other.

"Trace, can't we just move your father?" Ari asked. "Can't we take him someplace warm? Kendra and I will—"

"NO!" King Crag yelled from the floor. His outburst was followed by his coughing and gasping for air. "I will not leave!"

Trace tried to calm his father. Ari and Kendra stepped outside to talk.

"I don't think he's going to live much longer," Ari said. "We have to do something."

"I don't get it," Kendra said. "Why do the Trolls want to destroy the tundra? There aren't any trees. It's really cold and dark all winter. You'd think the Trolls would love it here."

"I think the tundra helps to clean the world's air or water," Ari said. "Otherwise, the Trolls would leave it alone."

"Do you think the Trolls know that King Crag is weakened by the cold?" Kendra asked. "Do you think that's why they came here?"

"I don't know," Ari said. "Maybe this is just a good place for them to attack."

"Attack?" Kendra said.

The word was still hanging in the air, when Ari and Kendra heard an unusual sound. It was in the distance, outside the walls of the village. It started as a rumble but grew louder. The ground shook.

"What is that?" Ari asked.

Trace poked his head out from the house. "Oh, no," he said, looking off toward the sound. "I was afraid of this."

The noise was close now. It came from just on the other side of the village wall. Then, suddenly, it stopped.

A Giant Beast

Trace and the kids ran to the wall. When they reached it, Trace paused, facing the stones. His lower body stayed inside the village as he slowly leaned forward and his upper body disappeared through the wall.

He was trying to peek at what lay on the other side of the wall. When Trace pulled his head back in, Kendra gasped.

"Oh, my," she said.

Trace's head was covered in a sticky green slime. It oozed down his body. It

dropped to the ground in huge globs. Trace looked as if he might throw up.

"That's gross," Ari said. "What *is* that?"

Trace was now on his hands and knees. He tried to wipe his face with one hand while holding his stomach with the other. The smell was making him gag.

"Mammoth slime," he said. "It drooled on me."

"Mammoth?" Kendra asked. "Do you mean a real, live woolly mammoth?"

Trace nodded.

"What in the world is a woolly mammoth doing outside the village wall?" Ari asked.

Trace wiped the last of the slime from his face and fought his way back to his feet. He could choke out only one word: "Trolls!"

Kendra turned to Ari. "What are the Trolls going to do with a woolly mammoth?" she asked quietly.

"I'm not sure," Ari said. "Maybe this time instead of destroying the biome right away, the Trolls are planning to destroy the Imps first. With the Imps gone, the Trolls can take control of the biome and destroy it more easily."

Kendra nodded. "So the Trolls led the Imps to the tundra, where they somehow knew King Crag would be weak," she said. "And while the Imps are worrying about their king, the Trolls plan to attack them to gain control of the tundra biome."

"After that, they can destroy other biomes, too," Ari said.

Trace overheard Ari and Kendra talking. "The Trolls already *have* attacked," he said. "Last night, they pounded on the village wall until it cracked. That is how the cold air got through the village walls. We knew Trolls were too weak to crack the wall alone. But we were not sure how they had done it. Until now."

"OK, Ari. What are we going to do?" Kendra asked.

"I have an idea," Ari said. "But we'll need a lot of help."

6

Plan of Attack

Night was only moments away. Darkness meant that the Trolls would soon be safe to rise to the surface of the tundra.

Trace took care of his father in the small house while Ari and Kendra talked about their plan outside. The plan would require help from a number of the Imps. Kendra left to find some volunteers. Ari went back inside the house to talk to Trace.

When Ari opened the door, he saw Trace crouched near the king. Ari placed his hand on Trace's shoulder and said, "We have a plan."

He led Trace outside, away from the house. As they walked, they passed Kendra and a handful of Imps. "Kendra," Ari said, "Trace and I need to talk. Please take your volunteers and go stay with the king. Make sure he is kept warm."

Kendra nodded, and Ari and Trace walked toward the village wall. Ari asked a lot of questions about the woolly mammoth and what the Trolls might be planning.

"Most likely," Trace said, "they plan to storm the walls of the village. They will use the mammoth to knock the walls down. Once the Trolls are inside, we will be unable to stop them, especially with my father being so ill."

"Can we strengthen the walls?" Ari asked. "You must have the power to make those walls stronger somehow."

"We can do many things," Trace said. "But we cannot stop a mammoth from destroying the walls of our village."

Ari opened his mouth to ask another question, but a rumble from outside the village walls stopped him. Now the growls and groans of the Trolls could be easily heard. Trace turned to face Ari.

"I thought you said you had a plan," Trace said. "What is it? We must do something quickly. Quickly! I can hear the Trolls outside the walls! If we do not do something now, all will be lost!"

Ari struggled to find words. "I … um … I, I do," he said. "I do have a plan."

Just then, a scream split the air. It was Kendra. The entire Imp village fell silent once again as the door to King Crag's tiny house burst open.

"The king is dead!" Kendra screamed.
"King Crag is dead!"

Heavy Hearts

Trace fell to his knees, his head in his
hands. His sobs could be heard throughout
the village. Ari bent down to comfort him.

Another Imp ran to the front of the king's house. He carried a long case and was hurrying to put on a special purple robe. He opened the case and pulled out a large, curved horn. Then he began to play, loudly but slowly. It was a sad song that signaled the death of King Crag.

Imps rushed from behind shrubs and rocks and out of their homes. They gathered in the village square. They were shocked by the news. They spoke quietly or not at all. Many of the Imps cried, holding each other for comfort as well as for warmth.

Ari watched and waited. He wasn't sure exactly what would happen now. But he knew he would have to be ready to act quickly. He noticed that the sound from outside the walls—the sound of the Trolls— had quieted. Ari stayed with Trace, helping to comfort his tiny friend.

Hours passed. Finally, four Imps appeared from inside the house. They each held a corner of a wooden casket. Purple and gold robes were draped across it.

The other Imps parted as the casket was carried toward the village wall. They bowed and dropped to one knee, paying respect to their fallen king. The Imps lowered the casket as it reached Ari and Trace. Trace stood and placed his hand on it.

Ari and Trace let the casket pass, then followed behind it. When the Imps reached the village wall, Trace stopped them.

"I know we must take my father back to his birthplace," Trace said. "But if we exit through the wall here, the Trolls will see that the king is dead. Their attack will be fast and complete."

"Trace," Ari said, "the Trolls know. The horn and the cries of the Imps have already alerted them."

Trace nodded. He turned to face the Imps around him. They were all looking to him for leadership. That's when Trace realized that he was now the king.

"Let us all return to the birthplace of King Crag," Trace said. "We shall see that he gets a proper burial. We shall fight the Trolls another day."

The first two Imps carried the casket through the wall. Trace held Ari's hand, and they went through behind it. Hundreds of Imps followed.

The Trolls watched in silence as the Imps then lifted into the air and flew off. Trace,

still holding Ari's hand tightly, flew right behind the casket.

As the last Imp leapt into the air, a cry rose from the Trolls. The last sound the Imps heard as they flew away was the woolly mammoth crashing through the village wall.

A New Life

Kendra stayed behind in the village, hidden
in some bushes. She held a very valuable
piece of cargo wrapped in blankets against

her. She shuddered against the cold. But she worried more about the approaching Trolls.

A mighty blast from the woolly mammoth took down the village wall. Dozens of Trolls rushed in, holding torches above their heads. They ran in all directions and sniffed at the air. Some of them passed near Kendra, but none of them was able to find her.

Kendra was amazed that the Trolls could smell anything besides their own bad odor. They drooled as they stomped around the village. The knuckles of their twisted hands scraped on the ground.

"Burn the houses!" the Troll king shouted. "Once the Imp village is destroyed, we will melt the tundra!"

He laughed loudly. His war party put their flaming torches on the houses of all of the villagers.

When the Troll king came to King Crag's house, he handed a torch to the Troll queen.

"Here, my lovely," he said. "Set the house of the Imps' king on fire. Tomorrow you will be Queen of the Tundra!"

He howled with laughter as she took the flaming torch from him.

"But it won't be the tundra anymore!" the Troll queen yelled.

She lowered the torch to the bottom of the house. In just a few seconds, the wall was on fire. Soon, the tiny house was a pile of ash.

"Hurry! It's almost sunrise," the Troll king yelled. "All of you, get underground. Start the fires! We'll warm the tundra from below!"

In a flash, the Trolls were back below ground. The village was destroyed.

As the sun broke over the eastern sky, Kendra began to feel the heat from below. She heard the crackles of melting ice all around her. She smiled.

She crawled out from the bushes, carrying the valuable cargo against her chest. She searched for the warmest spot on the ground and quickly found it.

The ice was nearly gone. There, Kendra laid the bundle of blankets.

Meanwhile, Ari, Trace, and the Imps arrived at King Crag's birthplace. Quietly and calmly, they laid the casket on the stump of a large tree. Trace removed the

robes from the casket and prepared to open it. He needed to see his father one last time. He needed to say goodbye.

Ari grabbed Trace's hand, stopping him. "Allow me," he said as he unlatched the top of the casket. "I'm sorry, my little friend, but I had to trick you."

With that, Ari opened the casket. Trace stared blankly. It was empty!

Back in the village, there was a stirring in the blankets Kendra had laid on the warm ground. Out crawled a tiny figure.

King Crag was alive! The warmth had given him back his strength. Now he was ready to battle the Trolls.

As the ground around Kendra and the king melted, King Crag looked at the source of the heat. The huge fires the Trolls were burning below ground made some areas melt faster than others.

As King Crag made his plan, the Imps began to return. First to arrive was Trace. He rushed to hug his father.

King Crag told the Imps to dig in the areas where the ground was melting. The Imps directed the rushing water toward the holes in the ground. As the clear, clean water ran into the holes, the Imps could

hear the Trolls underground screaming. Huge, hissing clouds of steam rose from the holes as the fires sizzled and died.

Before long, the Trolls had all fled. The fires were put out. Once the heat was removed, the tundra began to return to its natural, frozen state. King Crag and the Imps moved quickly to start fixing the

 village walls. The Trolls' threat in the tundra was over. But the king didn't want to wait for the deep freeze to return.

Just as quickly, he told Trace to take Ari and Kendra home. But first, he called them to him.

"I am grateful to you for what you have done," said the king. "I am beginning to see that you are indeed special."

"You mean you believe—" Ari began.

King Crag raised his hand to silence Ari. "You must go now," he said.

Just as he had before, Trace took Ari and Kendra by their hands and walked them out of the village. In an instant, they had walked through the door and into the hallway outside Ari's bedroom.

Ari and Kendra were tired but full of questions. They wondered how the Trolls knew that the cold weakened King Crag. They wondered if they were the kids from the Imp Prophecy. They wondered where the Trolls would strike next. They wondered how many biome adventures still lay in front of them.

Trace held their hands tightly, unable to speak. Ari felt a small lump between his hand and Trace's. He knew what it was. Trace winked and disappeared back through the door.

Ari opened his hand and stared at the wadded-up paper Trace had left there.

Kendra lunged for it, laughing.

"It's my turn to open one of these," she said with a smile. She opened the paper, spread it flat, and looked at it. Written in backward letters it read:

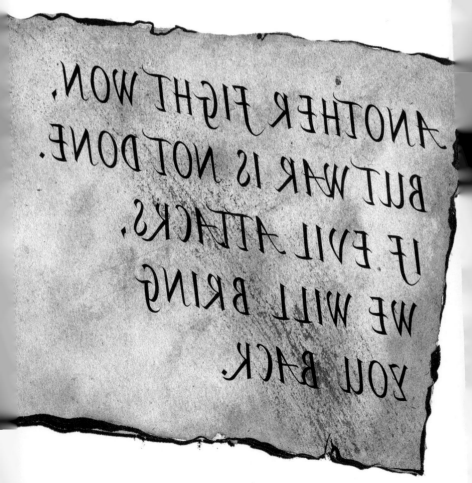

ANOTHER FIGHT WON.
BUT WAR IS NOT DONE.
IF EVIL ATTACKS,
WE WILL BRING
YOU BACK.

What Is the Tundra?

The tundra is the coldest biome in the world. Most of it lies in
the arctic and subarctic regions of the world.

The tundra has only two main seasons—summer and winter.
During the summer, the sun shines 24 hours a day. Temperatures
can reach 60 degrees Fahrenheit (16 degrees Celsius). The winter
months are dark and cold. The sun may not rise for weeks.
Winter temperatures can drop to minus 94 F (minus 70 C).

Tundra Plants and Animals

The tundra has a layer of frozen soil called permafrost. Permafrost
makes it impossible for trees to grow. Only low-growing plants,
such as moss and lichen, can live on the tundra. Tundra plants
have shallow roots and a short growing season.

The largest grazing animals on the tundra are musk oxen, caribou,
and reindeer. Other animals include arctic hares, lemmings, wolves,
snowy owls, and brown bears. Many bird species nest on the
tundra in the summer. They feed on black flies and mosquitoes.
But the birds fly south before the cold winter begins.

Why Is the Tundra Important?

The tundra is a carbon dioxide "sink." A "sink" is an area that
takes in more carbon dioxide than it releases.

Plants normally release carbon dioxide when they die and
decompose (break down). But because of the short summer and
the cold winter temperatures, tundra plants don't decompose. The
carbon dioxide gases are trapped in the permafrost.

Today, global warming is melting the permafrost. The trapped
carbon dioxide is being released into the air. Carbon dioxide is the
gas that causes global warming. As a result, several feet of the
tundra are lost every year, and a bad cycle is continued.

GLOSSARY ·
  arctic–having to do with the North Pole or the region
    around it
  biome–a large geographical area with its own distinct animals,
    plants, climate, and geography; there are six major biomes on
    Earth: desert, grassland (including savannas and prairies),
    ocean, rain forest, tundra, and wetlands
  carbon dioxide–a gas that people and animals breathe out
  equator–an imaginary line around the middle of Earth; it
    divides the northern half from the southern half
  permafrost–a layer of soil just below the surface that stays
    frozen year-round
  species–a group of animals or plants that has many things
    in common
  tundra–land with no trees that lies in the arctic regions

ON THE WEB
FactHound offers a safe, fun way to find Web sites related
to topics in this book. All of the sites on FactHound have
been researched by our staff.

  1. Visit *www.facthound.com*
  2. Type in this special code: 1404836489
  3. Click on the FETCH IT button.

Your trusty FactHound will fetch the best sites for you!